To James. —L.R.

To Matt and Ebby. —C.C.

Copyright © 2000 Lion Publishing plc
Original edition published by Lion Publishing plc, Oxford, England.
All rights reserved.

Typeset in Baskerville MT Schlbk,
New Baskerville and Aunt Mildred.
Printed in Malaysia.

Library of Congress Cataloging-in-Publication Data
Rock, Lois, 1953-
I wonder why? / by Lois Rock ; illustrated by Christopher Corr.
p. cm.
Summary: A child wonders about nature and his place in it.
ISBN 0-8118-3169-8
[1. Spirituality—Fiction. 2. Stories in rhyme.] I. Corr,
Christopher, ill. II. Title.
PZ8.3.R58615 Iwe 2001
[E]–dc21   00-011438

Distributed in Canada by Raincoast Books
9050 Shaughnessy Street
Vancouver, British Columbia, V6P 6E5

10 9 8 7 6 5 4 3 2 1

Chronicle Books LLC
85 Second Street, San Francisco, California 94105
www.chroniclebooks.com/Kids

I Wonder Why

by Lois Rock

illustrated by
Christopher Corr

chronicle books · san francisco

I sit here, just thinking, just wondering why The sun comes each day and brings light to the sky.

And why, in the dawnlight, the clouds are all pink

And yet the sun's yellow: it's odd, don't you think?

I wonder why animals crawl, walk and run
While birds get to fly, which must be more fun!

And why is grass green and the flowers so bright?

If leaves really whispered, just what would they say?

And where does the wind go w h e n i t

blows away?

Why do the sky-flying clouds fall as rain—

Do they just want to dance in the sea once again?

If we could touch rainbows,
would red feel hot,

The green a bit cooler,

and the violet—

well, what?

and just

long

to

stand still?

Which way should we go and why are we here

On a planet that spins round the sun in a year?

What shall I do now my life has begun?
Which things make me happy?

Which things are most fun?

I sit here just thinking, just wondering why.

When earth cannot answer

I'll look to the sky.